I'm *Geronimo Stilton*'s sister. As I'm sure you know from my brother's bestselling novels, I'm a special correspondent for *The Rodent's Gazette*, Mouse Island's most famous newspaper. Unlike my 'fraidy mouse brother, I absolutely adore traveling, having adventures, and meeting rodents from all around the world!

The adventure I want to tell you about begins at Mouseford Academy, the school I went to when I was a young mouseling. I had such a great experience there as a student that I came back to teach a journalism class.

When I returned as a grown mouse, I met five really special students: Colette, Nicky, Pamela, Paulina, and Violet. You could hardly imagine five more different mouselings, but they became great friends right away. And they liked me so much that they decided to name their group after me: the Thea Sisters! I was so touched by that, I decided to write about their adventures. So turn the page to read a fabumouse adventure about the

THEA SISTERS!

Colette

She has a passion for clothing and style, especially anything pink. When she grows up, she wants to be a fashion editor.

Paulina

Cheerful and kind, she loves traveling and meeting rodents from all over the world. She has a magic touch when it comes to technology.

Violet

She's the bookworm of the group, and she loves learning. She enjoys classical music and dreams of becoming a famous violinist.

THE THEA SISTERS

Nicky
She comes from Australia and is very enthusiastic about sports and nature. She loves being outside and is always ready to get up and go!

Pamela
She is a great mechanic: Give her a screwdriver and she'll fix anything! She loves pizza, which she eats every day, and she loves to cook.

Do you want to help the Thea Sisters in this new adventure? It's not hard — just follow the clues!

When you see this magnifying glass, pay attention: It means there's an important clue on the page. Each time one appears, we'll review the clues so we don't miss anything.

**ARE YOU READY?
A NEW MYSTERY AWAITS!**

Thea Stilton

AND THE
MYSTERY IN PARIS

Scholastic Inc.

Published by Scholastic Inc., *Publishers since 1920*, 557 Broadway, New York, NY 10012. SCHOLASTIC and associated logos are trademarks and/or registered trademarks of Scholastic Inc.

ISBN 978-0-545-22773-5

Text by Thea Stilton
Original title *Mistero a Parigi*
Cover by Arianna Rea, Paolo Ferrante, and Ketty Formaggio
Illustrations by Arianna Rea, Paolo Ferrante, and Ketty Formaggio
Illustrations by Maria Abagnale, Alessandro Battan, Fabio Bono, Pietro Dichiara, Barbara Di Muzio, Paolo Ferrante, Carlo Alberto Fiaschi, Claudia Forcelloni, Maria Rita Gentili, Daniela Geremia, Marco Meloni, Elena Mirulla, Roberta Pierpaoli, Arianna Rea, and Federico Volpini
Graphics by Paola Cantoni and Michela Battaglin

Special thanks to Beth Dunfey
Translated by Julia Heim
Interior design by Kay Petronio

32 31 30   21 22 23

Printed in the U.S.A.   40
This edition first printing 2019

A ROSE FOR THEA

It was one of those *HOT* spring mornings when you can tell summer's about to begin. I was out on my balcony, watering my flowers and enjoying the *SUN*. My garden was blooming beautifully! I have quite the GREEN paw, if I do say so myself.

Oh, I almost forgot to introduce myself. My name is THEA STILTON. My brother is *Geronimo Stilton*, the famouse publisher of **THE RODENT'S GAZETTE**. I am a special correspondent for his newspaper.

Out of the corner of my eye, I noticed a **DELIVERY TRUCK**

stopping on the street outside my building. A moment later . . .

Ding-dong! Ding-dong!

The doorbell started to ring.

"Is anyone home?" someone shouted SHRILLY. "Open up! I can't wait here all day!"

It was the unmistakable squeak of **Mercury Whale**, MOUSEFORD ACADEMY'S mailmouse. Mouseford is a famous school on Whale Island. I studied there as a mouseling, and had recently worked there as a visiting professor.

I scurried to open the door. But when I flung it open, instead of Mercury I saw a SplenDid bunch of roses!

"Where should I put it?" came a muffled squeak from inside the rosebush. "Hello? I'm getting pricked by thorns here! Where should I put it?"

I noticed that the bush had two SKiNNY legs sticking out from under it. I could barely see the tip of Mercury's snout peeking out between the flowers.

"Come in, Mercury!" I said, opening the door wide. "Right this way."

I led him out to the balcony. There was an empty corner that was just perfect for the wonderful rosebush.

But who was it from? Before I had a chance

to ask Mercury, he was scampering off to catch the ferry back to **Whale Island**. He was out the door faster than a hungry cat at feeding time.

It was then that I noticed a YELLOW card sticking out of the bush.

Sweets for the sweet. Roses for our beloved Thea! xoxo, the Thea Sisters

"What kind mouselings!" I exclaimed. The bush was a GIFT from my favorite students, five mouselings I had gotten to know at Mouseford when I had returned to teach there. They had excelled in my course on investigative journalism and had even helped me solve a mystery. They'd decided to name themselves after me: the THEA SISTERS.

I **turned** the card over to see if there was anything written on the back, and I found this message: *Check your e-mail. We've sent you the story and photos from our latest adventure—in Paris!*

I hurried over to my **LAPTOP** and turned it on. Sure enough, there was a long, juicy e-mail from *Colette*, *Nicky*, *Pamela*, PAULINA, and **Violet**!

So I made myself **comfortable** in my lawn chair, propped up my laptop on my knees, and began to read.

The five mouselings' latest adventure had started over school break.

As I read the first paragraph, I knew that I had found the perfect story for a new book. The title?

THE MYSTERY IN PARIS!

VACATION!

Spring had arrived at Mouseford Academy. The AIR was warm and fragrant, blowing the scent of flowers and freshly cut grass into the classrooms. Spring fever had broken out across campus. The students had a two-week vacation, and the air was abuzz with excitement.

The THEA SISTERS (Colette, Nicky, Pamela, PAULINA, and **Violet**) had their bags packed and plane tickets ready. For once, they weren't leaving to solve a mystery somewhere in the world. They were going on a nice, LOOONG vacation to Paris.

Colette was their host. She was famouse for overpacking, but this time she was the only one without luggage. She carried a heart-shaped purse and nothing else. Why?

Because the mouselings were headed straight for her house, and she was looking forward to visiting her **OVERFLOWING** closets. And Colette was determined to head out on a shopping *MARATHON* once they arrived in Paris!

The stairway of the academy's dorm was filled with happy squeaking. The students were chatting about their vacation.

Even *Octavius de Mousus*, the headmaster, was **BEAMING**. He said good-bye to his students with a broad smile. "Enjoy your vacation!"

The **Whale Island** port was crowded. Everyone was boarding the ferry bound for Mouse Island, including the THEA SISTERS.

As the ferry was sailing off, **Mercury whale** and his brothers broke into a verse of Whale Island's traditional farewell song, "Hymn for a Happy Return."

May your journey be a breeze,
Rich with smiles and rich with cheese!
May your return be filled with delight.
We'll await your arrival day and night.
When you return, we'll all eat cheesecake.
But don't forget to bring us a keepsake!

PARIS IS BEAUTIFUL IN THE SPRING!

As Whale Island gradually became smaller and smaller on the horizon, the five mouselings felt their excitement grow and grow.

Pamela, Nicky, and Paulina had never been to Paris and were longing to see it.

Violet had been there as a MOUSELING with her parents, and it had stayed in her heart. Going back with her closest friends was a dream come true.

As for Colette, Paris was *her* city! She couldn't wait to play TOUR GUIDE for her friends.

When they reached

Mouse Island, the five friends made their way to the airport. After check-in, they got a SNACK at the café and waited CHEERFULLY for their flight to be called. It was so nice not to be rushing around! For once, there was no anxiety, no worrying. For the first time ever, the Thea Sisters were enjoying a totally relaxing trip together!

That is, an ALMOST totally relaxing trip. As soon as the plane took off, it hit a fierce STORM, and the plane began to bounce up and down.

"I feel like I'm riding on the back of a KANGAROO," cried Nicky, who was from Australia.

Pam nodded. "But not in a good way!"

"It's okay, just stay calm. Find a happy place, find a happy place, find a happy place . . . ," Colette repeated to herself. She had turned as pale as a slice of mozzarella.

"Are you okay, Colette?" asked Violet.

"No, I'm not okay! Nothing is okay!" Colette burst out. She was on the verge of tears. "I don't have an **UMBRELLA**, all my clothes will get wet, my hair will **FRIZZ** from the humidity, and *Paris* will seem so **UGLY** in the rain!"

Violet smiled and **HUGGED** her friend. "After some **shampoo**, your hair will be gorgeous. And after the rain, *Paris*

will be **more beautiful than ever**!"

As it turned out, Violet was **100 PERCENT** correct in her predictions!

Just as the plane began to descend, the clouds broke and the sun shone like a spotlight on the city. The rows of buildings seemed to SPARKLE from the rain, and a beautiful rainbow framed the whole scene.

"AMAZING!" exclaimed Pamela. Her eyes were glued to the city that stretched out before them.

"Now that's what I call a welcome sign!" cried Paulina, pointing to the rainbow.

"It's fabumouse!" cried Nicky.

Colette smiled happily. "You see? Paris is just like me. It loves making a dramatic entrance!"

Paris

Paris was founded by Celtic tribes in the third century BC on an island in the River Seine. This island was called Lutetia; today it is known as Île de la Cité, which means "Island of the City" in French.

Today Paris is an important economic center and an artistic and cultural metropolis. It is considered one of the most fascinating cities in the world because of its unique beauty and atmosphere.

AT THE TOP OF THE CITY OF LIGHT!

Colette guided the mouselings from Paris-Orly Airport to the center of the city.

First they boarded a bus, which took them to the subway station of Denfert-Rochereau. Then they went DOWN to the METRO — that is, the SUBWAY — and crossed the entire downtown area of Paris, arriving at Place des Abbesses.

As they CLIMBED the stairs of the METRO and peeked out into the luminous OPEN square, the mouselings were a little DISORIENTED. But Colette didn't give them a minute to get their bearings. "Backpacks on, mouselings! Let's go! Move those tails!" she instructed her friends with a smile.

Paris

Rouen

Amiens

St. Quentin

Reims

Place des Abbesses

Denfert-Rochereau

1. Sacré-Coeur Basilica
2. Gare du Nord (North Station)
3. Cité des Sciences et de l'Industrie (largest science museum in Europe)
4. Père-Lachaise Cemetery
5. Nôtre Dame Cathedral
6. Paris-Orly Airport
7. Eiffel Tower
8. Stade Roland Garros (French Open stadium)
9. Bois de Boulogne
10. Arc de Triomphe
11. Paris Opéra

Colette's parents didn't live in *Paris*. In fact, Colette had grown up in the town of Arles in Provence. But when Colette was in **high school**, she and her older cousin JULIE moved to Paris together while Colette's parents were traveling. Julie and Colette shared a small apartment. That was where the THEA SISTERS would be "living it up"

(Colette's words!) during their Vacation.

The mouselings scampered up a very narrow, very STEEP road. Then they climbed a stairway, and then ANOTHER, and ANOTHER STILL.

"Where are you taking us? To the top of the **Himalayas**?" Pamela asked, panting.

"We are at the **BUTTE MONTMARTRE**," explained Colette. "In French, *butte* means

SACRÉ-COEUR

The **Sacré-Coeur (Sacred Heart) Basilica** on Montmartre dominates most views of Paris. The basilica is pure white and remains so because it is made out of travertine, a stone that exudes white calcite. Construction on the church began in 1875 and ended in 1914.

'hill.' It is the **highest** point in all of Paris!"

The mouselings spotted the white dome of the Sacré-Coeur Basilica high above them.

At last, they arrived at Colette's building. It was **TALL** and narrow, with an old-fashioned feel to it. On the top floor, there was a BALCONY filled with multicolored roses.

"Colette!" shouted a CLEAR squeak above their heads. It was Julie. She was waving her paws so they would **SEE** her. Her blonde bobbed hair peeped between the roses.

20

Inside the building, another **steep** staircase awaited the mouselings. Colette's apartment was on the top floor.

Montmartre

The two neighborhoods of Montmartre and Montparnasse in Paris are on opposite ends of the city. Both were, at different times, the heart of artistic life in Paris.

MONTMARTRE is a name of uncertain origin. Some believe that it comes from *Mons Martis*, which means "Mountain of Mars" in Latin. (Mars was the Roman god of war.) Others think it comes from *Mons Martyrum*, because it was here that some Christian martyrs died.

Montmartre was a hillside village that was absorbed by Paris during the second half of the nineteenth century. It soon became a center for painters, poets, and singers. Even today in the Place du Tertre, the main square in Montmartre, many painters work on the street.

Place du Tertre

Montparnasse

MONTPARNASSE

In the early twentieth century, artists started abandoning Montmartre in favor of the cheaper studio spaces available in Montparnasse, on the southern side of Paris. Montparnasse quickly became the new heart of artistic Paris. Great artists like Modigliani, Picasso, and Brancusi and writers like Céline, Joyce, and Proust made the neighborhood famous all over the world.

Today Montparnasse is one of the most modern neighborhoods in Paris. The only skyscraper in Paris, the Tour Montparnasse, which is hated by many French people, has become its symbol.

Tour Montparnasse

JULIE,
TRÈS JOLIE!*

Colette opened the door to the apartment and ushered her friends in.

JULIE ran to greet them. "Welcome!" She squeezed Colette TIGHTLY in her arms and rushed to grab Paulina's bag. "Did you have a good trip? You must be exhausted, poor things! And hungry, too! The cheese on those airplanes is always moldy. You must be starving!"

Julie spoke very quickly. She was a small mouse, but she seemed to have boundless energy. She kissed each mouseling on the cheek, then led them into the living room.

Pamela, Violet, Nicky, and Paulina were too exhausted to be polite. They collapsed

* *Jolie* is French for "pretty."

onto two comfy couches, sighing with relief.

Julie and Colette disappeared into the kitchen and came back a few moments later with a tray of cold drinks and cheese and crackers.

"Snacks? Juice?" Julie offered. "Don't be shy. Have something to eat; then you can rest. Please make yourselves at home. Colette and I will prepare LUNCH!"

The apartment was very comfortable and full of light. There wasn't much furniture, but there were a lot of pictures and a wonderful arrangement of roses at the center of the table.

"This place is lovely!" said Pam.

"I would never have imagined that a modern apartment like this would be inside such an OLD building," commented Paulina.

"My grandmother always says that appearances can be deceiving," said Violet, "and this is proof that old proverbs are always right!"

Colette peeked out of the kitchen. "Do you think you can make it up another flight of stairs?" she asked teasingly. With that, she pushed a button on the wall. A panel on the ceiling, which no one had noticed before, slid open silently. A WOODEN stairway unfolded

down toward them.

"**WOW!**" exclaimed Nicky in admiration. "What other tricks do you have in this place?"

"No more tricks!" **ANSWERED** Colette, inviting them to climb up. "My room is up here. The **FOLDING** staircase makes the rooms much more spacious!"

"What a **WONDERFUL discovery**!" said Paulina as she started up the stairs. She was

WOW!

very **curious**. *I bet the room is painted* **PINK***!* she thought.

When she emerged at the top, Paulina was squeakless. Nicky, Pam, and Violet, who had followed her, were, too.

"**Well?** Don't you have anything to say?" asked Colette.

"We . . . are *breathless*," sighed Pamela.

"And not just because of the stairs!" Nicky said, laughing.

Colette's room was ENCHANTING! It had once been an attic, and it had a sloping ceiling and exposed ceiling beams. The wallpaper was pale **pink** with fuchsia **stripes**. The canopy bed had light curtains that were a little brighter than the walls. The blanket that covered the bed was dark blue with tiny pink designs.

But the really **EXTRAORDINARY** thing was the view from the window: a sea of roofs and chimneys as far as the eye could see, and above them all was the dome of *Sacré-Coeur*!

From above, *Paris* was even more *magical*.

SHOP UNTIL YOU DROP!

Right after lunch, Julie had to leave her new friends and head off to **RATIZON'S FASHION ACADEMY**. She was studying there to become a *fashion designer*!

Unlike Colette and the other mouselings, Julie wasn't on **vacation**. At her school, it was tradition for mice who were about to graduate to present their clothing collections at the end of the school year. That year, the final fashion show would be held under the *Eiffel Tower*!

In those last few days before the show, all the students were **frantically** putting the finishing touches on their collections. The fashion show would be viewed by some of the most FAMOUSE designers in the world!

In the meantime, the THEA SISTERS had a full afternoon planned.

"I can't wait to see Paris!" exclaimed Paulina. She reached out and **squeezed** Colette's paw. "And it's going to be just fabumouse to have you as our tour guide!"

Colette, Nicky, Pamela, PAULINA, and **Violet** headed toward the city center on the Metro. "The **RIVER SEINE** runs through the middle of Paris," Colette explained. "The two sides of the city are called the Right Bank and the Left Bank. Let's start off on the Left Bank!"

"Why?" asked Violet.

Colette LAUGHED. "Why? That's easy. The **Left Bank** has all the most

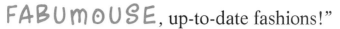

FABUMOUSE, up-to-date fashions!"

With that, Colette dragged her friends into a **WHIRLWIND** of shopping.

Everything was *gorgeous*. And though Violet would have preferred to be at a **mouseum**, she had a lot of fun trying on the latest styles.

"You're right, Colette," Paulina sighed. "*Paris* really is the fashion capital of the **WORLD**!"

After a few hours, Nicky looked at her watch. "Uh-oh, mouselings, look at the time! We **promised** Julie we'd meet her at the academy."

"You're right!" said Colette, jumping up in alarm. She looked around ~~anxiously~~. Then she spotted a bus stop. "Come on! We'll be there faster than you can say '**toasted Brie** on **baguettes**!'"

RATIZON'S FASHION ACADEMY

Finding the academy was **easy**. But once inside, finding Julie was **veeeeeery** complicated.

The mouselings were immediately caught up in the **comings and goings** of all the ***STRESSED-OUT*** students. Everyone

RATIZON'S FASHION ACADEMY
CLASS SCHEDULE

8:00–9:00	Yoga (to stimulate creativity)
9:00–11:00	Design on mannequins
11:00–1:00	Sewing class and decoration application (sequins, patchwork, embroidery)
1:00–2:00	Lunch break
2:00–3:30	History of fashion
3:30–5:00	Seminar: Finding a good idea in fashion. Featured squeaker: Monsieur Ratizon
5:00–6:00	How to organize a fashion show

knew Julie, but no one knew where she was.

Violet saw two ASIAN mouselings who were identical **twins**. They had strangely cut hair: short on one side and long on the other, half orange and half blue. She asked them if they knew where Julie was.

"JULie?" one of them asked. "She went to see the director!"

"Yeah, she's always COMPLAINING about something!" commented the other twin.

"Julie!" called Colette, noticing her cousin emerge from an elevator.

Julie was talking to a professor. She had a TENSE look on her snout. The teacher had a PAW on her shoulder and was squeaking very gENTLY, "You are one of the best students in the academy, Julie. It's only natural that some of the students are jealous of you. You're talented! But this is the fashion world: It's CUT or BE CUT." The professor smiled and left.

"What happened, Julie?" asked Colette.

Hugo Le Blanc

"Who was that rodent?"

"That was Professor Hugo Le Blanc. He teaches the *history of fashion*," Julie answered. "He was trying to **lift** my spirits."

"What's wrong?" asked Pam.

Julie rubbed her snout sadly. "Someone **snuck** into my studio and **went through** everything. And it wasn't the first time!" she finished, turning **red**.

"Did they **STEAL** anything?" Pam wanted to know.

"No," said Julie. "At least, I don't think anything is **missing**. But it's not really about stealing my belongings . . . it's my **IDEAS** that are valuable! Luckily, I left my **LAPTOP** at home. That's where all my notes and **designs** are."

CAFÉ FLORIEN

"Mouselings, the stress of this fashion show is making my head spin!" Julie said with a sigh. "I need to relax."

"Good for you, Julie!" said Colette approvingly. "Why don't we go shopping?"

Violet shook her head. "Oh, no, a cup of green tea would be better, with some jasmine. That's what Julie needs."

"What are you crazy rodents squeaking about?" Pamela burst out. "Shopping? Tea? Uh-uh. It's time to eat! You need some PIZZA in your stomach, Julie! Some delicious melted Parmesan is just what you need to perk you up."

Julie smiled. "You're right, Pam! I'm hungry. Dinner is just what we need!"

So, together, the six mouselings left the

FASHION ACADEMY. Outside, the sunset colored the roofs pink. Paris was even more spectacular at twilight.

They arrived in front of a restaurant that was covered in flowers. There were flowers everywhere!

Pamela thought Julie was playing a JOKE on them. "You're not going to make us eat flowers, are you, Julie?" she asked, laughing.

"*Mais oui!** Of course!*" Julie answered. "Cooking with flowers is *in style* in Paris!"

Pamela was **squeakless**. Was Julie kidding?

Pam, Nicky, Paulina, and Violet gathered around the menu posted on the door.

Pamela read the menu carefully, but she still couldn't believe it.

"I bet there's some sort of PLAY on words

Today's specials
Rice with red roses
Sauteed medley
from the garden
Daisies in vinaigrette
Violets and vanilla
ice cream with candied
rose petals

* *Mais oui* means "oh, yes" in French.

here that I don't understand," she whispered to Nicky. "There's no way they can make rice with roses!"

Nicky shrugged. "I've eaten stranger things at home in Australia, so I'm game."

Inside, the little group found a table. After a few minutes, the waiter brought them a plate covered in red **petals**.

Pamela was seriously tempted to scamper out and go find a good old-fashioned pizza. "The Brie must've slipped off the **CHEF'S baguette**," she murmured. But her friends seemed to be enjoying the food, and she didn't want Julie to think she was **RUDE**. So she closed her eyes and took a TINY bite of rice with a petal on top.

"It's deeee-licious!!!!" yelled Pam in surprise. "Who knew flowers could be so **tasty**?"

A STROLL ALONG THE SEINE

The evening was warm, and the air smelled sweet. Julie was feeling much better after a good dinner and a pep talk from her friends. It was *enchanting* to take a nice stroll along the Seine. The water from the river reflected the **LIGHTS** of the city, looking like a silk *ribbon* studded with *paillettes.*

"Look! It's the **EIFFEL TOWER**!" cried Nicky. She

* In French, *paillettes* means "sequins."

The River Seine divides the city into two parts. On the
Right Bank (the Rive Droite), there are many businesses and
museums, like the stock market and the Louvre. The Left Bank
(the Rive Gauche) is home to the more intellectual side of
Paris, including Sorbonne University and the Latin Quarter.
Thirty-eight bridges and three boardwalks cross the Seine.

was thrilled to see it up close. The famouse tower was lit up for the evening, and it seemed to sparkle against the night sky.

Julie nodded. "That's where our fashion show is going to be held."

"**Fabumouse!**" exclaimed Colette.

"**Ratastic!**" Nicky echoed.

"And you will present your designs?" Paulina wanted to know.

"Not just me," explained Julie. "All the students who will graduate this year from the **ACADEMY** will show their collections. It's part of our final exam."

"How *THRILLING*!" exclaimed Violet.

"I'm calling my collection **TrEAsurE HuNt**," said Julie. "Each collection is supposed to have a *theme*. I was inspired by an **OLD MAP** that I stumbled on."

"And that's why you called the whole

collection **TrEAsurE HUnt**!" Pamela said. "What a **stylish** idea! I would definitely buy a jacket with that name on it."

Julie smiled. Then she took a package out of her backpack and gave it to Colette. "I wish I had a gift for all of you, but I ran out of time! This is a present for Colette. I designed it with her in mind."

"For me?" exclaimed Colette, looking surprised and pleased. She began opening

the package and pulled out a soft pink silk shawl. "It's just **GORGEOUS**!" she said admiringly, pulling it across her shoulders.

"Hey, it's really a **MAP**!" exclaimed Pamela, observing the design on the fabric.

"What does it **mean**?" asked Violet curiously.

"I don't know," answered Julie. "I found this **OLD MAP** in a book, and I just **LOVED** it. So I thought I would use it to design my fabrics for the end-of-the-year fashion show!"

"What a great idea," said Paulina. "It's *très chic**!"

* In French, *très chic* means "very stylish."

BREAKING AND ENTERING . . . WITHOUT THE BREAK-IN!

The next morning, JULie left early for the **FASHION ACADEMY**. The THEA SiSTERS sat down to a breakfast of cheese croissants and discussed their plans for the day.

"There are so many incredible **mouseums** we need to visit!" Violet cried. "The Louvre, the Musée d'Orsay . . ."

Nicky shook her head. "Uh-uh. Oh, no. We spent all day yesterday inside. I need some fresh air! Let's go to a park."

Colette looked stunned. "**WHAT DO yOU MEAN?** We still have all the boutiques on the Right Bank to visit!"

Colette turned to Pam and Paulina.

"No way," said Pam. "My paws are destroyed after all that scampering around we did yesterday."

Paulina nodded. "And I've already spent all the money I put aside for shopping."

Before the bickering could continue, the phone rang. Colette scurried to answer it. "*Allô?* Oh, hi, Julie . . . WHAT?!"

Colette started squeaking *French* so rapidly that *Nicky*, *Pamela*, PAULINA, and **Violet** were able to understand only one word: *volé*.

"*Volé* means '**STOLEN**,' right?" Paulina asked.

Violet nodded.

Finally, Colette hung up. "Someone stole Julie's collection! Last night someone **broke into** the academy and took all of her clothes for the *fashion show*!"

"**ALL** of them?" Pamela, Nicky, and Paulina asked in unison.

"And only hers? What about the other students' work?" asked Violet in **shock**.

"All of them. And only Julie's clothes!" confirmed Colette. "Here's the interesting part: Whoever it was didn't have to **BREAK** open the door or windows to get in!"

"We've got to go meet Julie!" cried Nicky.

Colette led the way. When they reached the academy, they met with all the **HUSTLE AND BUSTLE** they had encountered the previous day. Violet spotted the twins and asked them to take the THEA SISTERS to Julie's studio right away.

Julie was alone and in **tears**. Her studio was crowded with fabric, sketches of her designs, books on fashion, and spools and spools of THREAD and *ribbon*. But all the

The thief took only Julie's clothes, leaving all the other students' work behind. Strange, very strange . . .

hangers on which her collection had hung were EMPTY.

"Where are the P O L I C E?" Colette demanded.

Julie wiped a tear from her snout. "The officers asked a few questions; then they left. They were only here for a few minutes."

"That's it?" Pamela was *dumbfounded*.

"They promised they would look into it," Julie explained. "It's just some clothes made by a student, not exactly a PRICELESS TREASURE. The police don't care that much about something so unimportant!"

"What?" Colette BLURTED OUT. "So they left without **questioning** witnesses? Without taking PAWPRINTS? They didn't check everyone's alibi?"

Julie smiled sadly. "Everyone's? Do you know how many rodents there are in the

academy? More than **TWO HUNDRED**! Plus, the police think the case is already solved. They say that it's just a ratfight. 'Jealousy among students,' they told me."

"I have an idea!" Violet interrupted. "I saw a tearoom right next door. Let's go there and plan our next move."

Julie was puzzled. "Our next move? I don't understand. . . ."

"If the P O L I C E can't do anything, we'll have to take matters into our own paws!" Paulina explained.

"Leave it to us! We'll get your collection back!" Pamela declared.

"And if we don't do it in time for the fashion show . . . ," Nicky began.

"Then we aren't the THEA SISTERS!" all five mouselings said together.

CLUE REVIEW

The *sweet* smell of jasmine tea helped calm P O O R Julie's nerves.

"Let's start with the most OBVIOUS clue," Colette began. "The thief didn't have to FORCE the door or the windows open to get in."

"So he or she must have had a copy of the KEYS. And he must have known the

CLUE!

C O D E to deactivate the academy's alarm system," Pamela continued.

Julie nodded. "That's what the police said, too. They said that it had to be someone inside the **ACADEMY**."

"Of course!" agreed Violet. "Everyone's a **SUSPECT**. We shouldn't count anyone out."

"The other students have a motive: jealousy. But what about the teachers and the rest of the staff?" asked Nicky.

"It's so frustrating!" Colette said. "We don't know if the other rodents had motives or not because they weren't questioned!"

"But you have a plan to question them, right?" asked Violet with a sly grin.

Colette winked. "**Leave everything in my paws, Julie!**"

Did you catch that? If the thief didn't force his or her way through the door, it means he or she must have had the keys!

COLETTE, PRIVATE INVESTIGATOR

All it took was a wig, glasses, a suit, a blouse, and a briefcase. In this simple disguise, Colette was unrecognizable!

She entered the academy with a notepad in paw and started ROAMING around, searching for clues. Introducing herself as a journalist was enough to get her MAXIMUM cooperation from all the students, who were longing to get publicity for their collections.

Colette

Wanda said she suspected **Wei** and **Mei**, the **TWINS**. "All those two know how to do is copy! Neither of them could design a dress to save her cheese. I bet they're the ones who stole Julie's designs."

Fernando, on the other paw, suspected Wanda. "She's jealous of Julie! Actually, she's jealous of everyone, because she doesn't have an original idea in her head. Have

FERNANDO

WEI AND MEI

WANDA

you seen her collection for the *fashion show*? It's simply hideous!"

Leon Paella, a student from Spain, had a different suspect in mind. "I don't want to accuse anyone, but Fernando would do anything (let me repeat: ANYTHING) to get a prize in the show!"

The most imaginative opinion came from **Wei** and **Mei**.

SALLY

JEAN

MADELINE

LEON PAELLA

EVELYN

TOBIAS

"Poor Julie! Her collection was a **disaster**!" said **Wei**.

"We think she's **faking** the robbery so she won't be embarrassed at the fashion show!" concluded **Mei**.

What a poisonous environment! thought Colette. She shook her head sadly.

Just then, she saw a shadow on the front wall. Colette turned to check it out, but it was only the curtain moving. The **window** had been left open.

Hmmm, Colette thought. *If this window was left open last night, then* **ANYONE** *could have gotten in!* She sighed. Tracking down the culprit was going to be harder than finding a slice of **GOUDA** hidden in a cheese shop.

A DOUBLE DISGUISE!

Meanwhile, Pamela and Nicky had a different approach to solving the MYSTERY. It was possible the thief hadn't taken Julie's designs very far. Maybe he or she had hidden them inside the ACADEMY. So they decided to SNOOP around a little.

Like Colette, they had found disguises. Their costumes were a lot simpler than Colette's: All they needed were a pair of

Nicky

Pamela

aprons, a broom, and a trash can to make them look like two cleaning mice.

The students weren't **SURPRISED** when two cleaning mice entered their studios and **WORKSHOPS** to empty the trash. It was the perfect way to see all the other collections.

Fernando had made clothes that looked like they were made out of **METAL**, as if they were buildings or cars. Leon Paella had designed suits that were more suitable for **robots** than for fur-and-bone models.

Wanda was inspired by **superheroes**: All her designs included tights and long, fluttery capes. And **Wei** and **Mei** had made clothing out of cut-up construction paper.

"Cute!" said Nicky.

"Yes . . . made out of paper . . . but what if it **RAINS**?" said Pamela. She was very practical. "Well, I don't like them at all! They look more uncomfortable than a **mousetrap** on the **tail**." She shuddered.

STROLLING DOWN THE BOULEVARDS

Violet and Paulina had offered to distract Julie while their friends were investigating. They asked her to be their guide along the streets of *Paris*. They tried to steer her far away from clothing stores and anyplace else that might remind Julie of her missing collection.

THE BIG BOULEVARD

In the middle of the nineteenth century, Paris still looked like a chaotic medieval city. Its streets were narrow, and the buildings were packed in too tightly. On the orders of Emperor Napoleon III, the urban planner **Baron Georges Eugène Haussmann** gave the city its present-day look. He demolished many of the old buildings, particularly on the Left Bank, and created wide boulevards, parks, and sweeping open spaces for Paris's squares. His grand boulevards are among the city's most noteworthy characteristics.

But when they passed a book stand along the Seine, Julie's eyes filled with tears.

"What's the matter, Julie?" asked Paulina, **alarmed**.

"I'm sorry!" said Julie. "I'm being silly, I know. It's just that this place reminds me of my collection."

"But why?" asked Violet, puzzled.

"This is where I found THE MAP!" explained Julie. "The one that gave me the idea for my Treasure Hunt collection.

You see, I came here one morning looking for inspiration. These **old** books are really **fascinating** to me. I said to myself, 'Who knows! Maybe I will find something that will **inspire** an original idea!'"

"And you did!" said Paulina.

Julie nodded. "Yes, I did, almost right away. I came across a **book** about *theatrical* costumes. I don't even know what drew me to it, but when I started leafing through it, I became **fascinated**. The costumes were so **GORGEOUS**!"

"And inside you found the map?" asked Violet.

"Yes! It was a real stroke of **LUCK**! But I didn't realize it right off. In fact, once I bought the book, I went back home to look through it. I sat down immediately and started turning the pages. Only at that point did I notice a page had **FALLEN** out. I grabbed it and saw that it had a strange D⊕ᶘⅰ⅗N on top. It didn't take me long to realize I was looking at a **MAP**!"

"It's amazing how you can find inspiration in even the most everyday things," Paulina said.

Julie nodded in agrEEmENt.

Violet took her by the paw. "Come on, mouselings, let's move those paws! There's still loads I want to see."

JULie smiled and wiped her snout. "Yes, let's shake a tail!"

IN THE BOIS DE BOULOGNE

The mouselings had agreed to meet for lunch in the enormouse *Bois de Boulogne* (Boulogne Woods) park. They wanted to compare notes about what they had learned from their investigations.

BOIS DE BOULOGNE
(Boulogne Woods)

After visiting London's famous Hyde Park, Emperor Napoleon III wanted to give Paris an extraordinary park of its own. From 1852 to 1870, the ancient forest of Rouvray was transformed into the Boulogne Woods under the supervision of Baron Haussman. The park is over 2,100 acres—more than twice the size of New York City's Central Park—with 142,000 trees, twenty-two miles of footpaths, and eighteen miles of horse-riding paths.

The afternoon was so **HOT** that it already felt like summer. So they decided to have a picnic next to the **lake**. They packed cheese, bread, and fruit: It was a regular rodent **feast**!

Julie, Violet, and Paulina were eager about hearing what their friends had discovered.

Unfortunately, the news wasn't good: No one had turned up anything interesting.

"It could have been any one of your classmates," said Colette. "Everyone seemed jealous of someone, and no one has an **alibi**

worth its **CHEDDAR**!"

"When there are **too many** suspects, it's like not having any," sighed Paulina, shaking her head.

"So basically, we haven't gotten anywhere," concluded Pam **sadly**.

Strangely, Julie seemed less disappointed than her friends were. "It is too nice a day to talk about such depressing things," she declared. "Let's enjoy our picnic! After we've eaten, we can BRAINSTORM a new plan."

So Pamela rented a rowboat and dragged Violet and Paulina on a trip around the lake. Nicky made friends with a group of rodents who were horseback riding around the park, and she joined them.

As for Julie and Colette, they stretched out

on the grass and chatted in the SUN. They REMINISCED about being little mouselings in school together, and a thousand other funny adventures they'd been through.

No one noticed that not too far away, someone was SPYING on them. . . .

CLUE!

Someone is spying on the Thea Sisters. Can you see where the spy is hiding?

ANOTHER BREAK-IN!

After their afternoon in the park, the mouselings stopped at a pizzeria—Pam's suggestion—for some dinner. By the time they got home, it was already dark, and there was an **ugly surprise** waiting for them.

As soon as they opened the door, they noticed the window was open and the glass was **shattered**. Julie's laptop was missing!

Before they could react . . .

CRAAAAASH!!!

The noise made them jump.

"The thief!" **screamed** Colette, running to the

window. When she looked out at the street, she saw a shadowy figure *dashing* up the stairs.

"My COMPUTER!" shouted Julie. Her laptop lay in fragments on the street below.

"The thief must have let it slip from his PAWS while he was getting away!" exclaimed Paulina.

THE THIEF!

Colette, JULIE, Nicky, Pamela, PAULINA, and **Violet** ran out to the street to recover what was left of the computer.

"**Moldy mozzarella!**" blurted Pamela. "Wasn't it enough for that slimy sewer rat to steal your clothes? Why did he have to steal your laptop, too?"

Julie felt broken into pieces, just like her computer.

As they headed back into the house, Violet said, "At least we have a new clue. The thief stole Julie's collection, but he wasn't really looking for the clothes—he was looking for *something else* that's linked to them! But what?"

"Yes, what could it be?" Colette echoed thoughtfully.

Violet was lost in thought for a minute. Then her eyes lit up. "Why didn't I realize it sooner?" she exclaimed, **smiling**. "The **MAP**!"

"The **MAP**?" the mouselings repeated together.

"Violet's right!" cried Julie. "The **THIEF** must be after the **MAP**!"

WHY DON'T WE REVIEW WHAT WE KNOW?

1. Julie's clothing collection was stolen from the fashion academy.

2. The thief took only Julie's clothes, which means that the other students' collections were not of interest.

3. The thief left no sign of a break-in at the academy. Therefore, he or she must have had keys, meaning that he or she must have been someone who belonged at the academy.

4. The thief tried to steal Julie's computer, too. Maybe the thief didn't find what he or she was looking for in Julie's clothes. So what was the thief looking for?

OLD MAPS, NEW TECHNOLOGY!

"I've got it!" continued JULie, who was finally connecting all the PiECES. "First the thief broke in to my studio. He was looking for the map, but he didn't find it. So he decided to steal the collection, hoping to put the MAP together by putting the CLOTHING together."

"So why did the thief want to steal your computer, too?" asked Pamela.

"When he couldn't find the real map, he probably hoped to find an ELECTRONIC scan on your computer!" Violet said. "When he tried to reconstruct the map with Julie's clothing, it wasn't complete! The LAST PIECE was missing."

Julie nodded. She went to get the shawl she'd GIVEN to Colette. "Of course! This is the missing P I E C E! Without the last piece, the collection was useless. The thief is missing the last piece of the MAP!"

"So he hoped Julie had SAVED a copy on her computer," Paulina concluded.

"That must be it," Julie said, nodding again. "Unfortunately, now my computer is in a thousand pieces, so no one can use it."

"Isn't there a BACKUP?" Paulina asked in disbelief.

Julie shrugged. "Nope, sorry. No copies."

"And the original MAP?" asked Violet, holding on to the last shred of hope.

"It's gone forever. I spilled a cup of HOT CHEESE on it when I was up late working on my collection, and it was completely destroyed."

Colette spread the shawl on the table, and all six mouselings gathered around.

"What does it represent?" asked Nicky.

"I don't have any idea," Julie replied.

"Look at all these SCATTERED letters!" Colette said, pointing each one out. "If we put them in the right order, perhaps they'll spell something!"

All of a sudden, Julie JUMPED to her feet. "G-a-r-n-i-e-r! I know what that means! The letters spell out the word *Garnier*! The Palais Garnier is the Paris Opera. It must be a map of the OPERA HOUSE!"

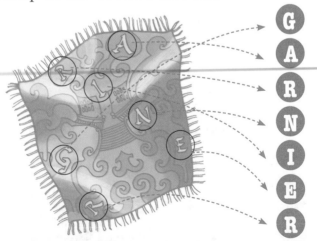

She ran to get the **book** in which she had found the map. The title was *Opera: Two Centuries of Costumes*.

Julie opened the book. It was an **old** volume, with **PRECIOUS** reproductions of stage **clothing** from the 1800s.

"It's a collection of costumes from the most famous OPERA productions!" Julie said.

Meanwhile, Paulina was sitting on the couch with her MousePhone. Suddenly, she asked Julie if she could use her printer.

"What have you found?" asked Pamela.

"You'll see!" answered Paulina, plugging her MousePhone into the printer.

TRZZ . . . a sheet of paper came out.

"This is the floor plan of the OPERA HOUSE," Paulina explained. "If the **MAP** is really a reproduction of this building, we should be able to find the part on the floor plan that corresponds to Colette's Shawl!"

Everyone gazed back and forth between the floor plan and the Shawl for a few minutes. Finally, Violet pointed her finger. "I've got it! This is the GRAND STAIRCASE. This is definitely it! Check it out."

The mouselings again peered back and forth between the two maps—Colette's shawl and the printout of the opera house's floor plan.

Of course! Colette's shawl was a copy of the GRAND STAIRCASE of the OPERA HOUSE!

"But what does it mean?" asked Nicky, looking **PUZZLED**. "Why would the thief be so desperate to learn about the OPERA

HOUSE? Couldn't he just download the floor plan, like Paulina did?"

"Of course he could," said Colette, nodding.

"There must be something special about this STAIRCASE," Violet said thoughtfully. "Maybe something's HIDDEN there."

"That's it!" cried Colette. "It's like the name of your collection, Julie! It must be a treasure of some kind!"

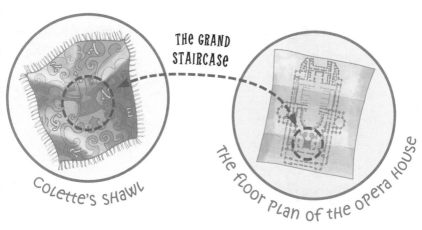

THE GRAND STAIRCASE

COLETTE'S SHAWL

THE FLOOR PLAN OF THE OPERA HOUSE

The Opera House

OPERA HOUSE

The construction of the Paris Opera House, or Théâtre de l'Opéra, was initiated by Napoleon III as part of his grand renovation plans for Paris. A competition was held to choose an architect, and an unknown young architect named Charles Garnier was the winner. The building's appearance is distinct; it blends several architectural styles and building materials.

The Opéra's grand staircase is one of the most famous parts of the theater. It is made of white, green, and red marble that came from quarries in France's colonies. The staircase has always been a place where famous Parisians have come to see and be seen.

THE GRAND STAIRCASE

Théâtre de l'Opéra

Construction on the Opéra began in 1861, but due to the enormous expenses involved, it wasn't finished until 1875, five years after the fall of Napoleon III. The theater opened on January 5, 1875.

THE GRAND FOYER

In a theater, the foyer is the space right outside the auditorium. It's the place where guests can relax and chat with fellow audience members before the show or during intermission. Before

THE GRAND FOYER

designing the Opéra, Garnier traveled throughout Europe, visiting its most famous theaters. While he was very traditional with the design for the stage and auditorium, he was much more innovative with the foyer. In the nineteenth century, most theaters had separate foyers—one for the nobility, one for the upper classes. Garnier overcame these divisions and created just one foyer, which was open to anyone who could afford the price of a ticket.

A REAL-LIFE TREASURE HUNT!

Pamela's eyes grew **wide**. "I think you're onto something, Colette. And if this map is so important to the thief, the **treasure** must be **REALLY** big!"

"You might be right," said Nicky, nodding. "But one thing's for sure: The thief won't be able to find it until he has the entire **MAP**."

"So what happens if the thief finds out that Colette's shawl is the last piece of the **PUZZLE**?" Violet asked slowly.

Colette stared at Violet. She knew what her friend was thinking. "**Oh no. Uh-uh! Don't even think about it!**" she shouted, clutching her **shawl**. "I don't know what your plan is, **Vi**, but you can't **TOUCH THIS**!"

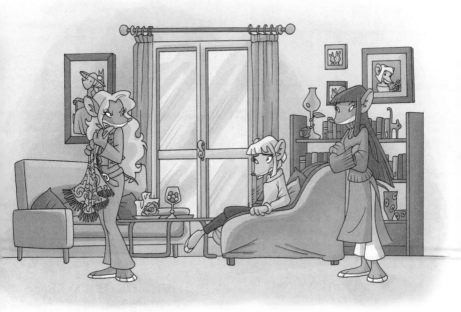

She **glared** at Violet, but as she did, she caught a glimpse of JULiE and began to soften. "Wh-what if the thief stole my shawl? I don't even want to think about it!"

"We'll get them with a **tracker**!" Paulina declared. "It's a good plan, Vi."

"What's a **tracker**?" Pam asked.

"It's a gadget that can send a signal to

reveal its location to a **COMPUTER** — like my MousePhone," explained Paulina.

Colette was starting to look interested in the plan. "**SO?** Then what?"

"So if we put a **tracker** on the Shawl and make sure the thief steals it, we would be able to find out where he is and follow the SiGNAL on my MousePhone!" Paulina said.

"Then we can follow him and find out what he's done with Julie's collection," Violet concluded.

"And the **THIEF** wouldn't know?" asked Colette.

"If the **tracker** is really, really SMALL, I can sew it into the hem of the Shawl!" interjected Julie.

"**Definitely!**" Paulina agreed. Then she looked at Colette. "Is that all right with you,

Colette? Are you willing to **sacrifice** your shawl to **CATCH THE THIEF**?"

Colette looked at Julie and smiled. "Of course! For JULie I would do this and more. There are only a few days until the fashion show, and we absolutely must find JULie's collection!"

TO CATCH A THIEF!

The THEA SISTERS' plan was set!

The next morning, Colette made a grand entrance at the **ACADEMY**. She was wearing the pink silk shawl, and she wanted everyone to notice it—especially the **THIEF**!

Colette sashayed toward the *secretary* of the **ACADEMY** and asked to squeak with the director about the end-of-the-year *fashion show*.

The **director** told Colette that the teacher who was in charge of the show was Professor Le Blanc.

With her shawl *flowing* behind her, Colette set out in search of the professor. She managed to cover the entire academy from top to bottom in the process.

Colette's distinctive shawl attracted STARES from students and teachers alike. If the THIEF was in the building (as the THEA SISTERS suspected), he was sure to notice and make his move.

A few minutes later, Professor Le Blanc entered the **ACADEMY**. Colette didn't waste any time. She RAN to meet him, calling out so everyone could hear, "Professor! Professor! My name is Colette. I'm Julie's cousin."

The professor looked at her with a smile. "Nice to meet you, Colette. What can I do for you?"

"I want to walk in the fashion show wearing this shawl!" Colette answered **LOUDLY**, doing a quick pirouette to show off the shawl. "Julie made it! It's part of her collection, TrEAsurE HuNt. It is the only PIECE that the THIEF was not able to steal, *because I had it*!"

All the rodents in the main hall stared at Colette, their mouths **HANGING** open.

Even Professor Le Blanc seemed STUNNED. "Well, this piece definitely has to be shown! Why don't you give it to me?"

"Oh, no," Colette said, taking a **STEP BACK**. "Impossible! The shawl is mine.

JULIe gave it to me. I will wear it for the **show**! There are too many **THIEVES** in this place. I don't feel **safe** leaving it. I will keep it with me always!"

"*There are rules and . . .*"

Professor Le Blanc was PERPLEXED. "I am afraid that is not allowed. There are **RULES** and . . ."

But he didn't have a chance to finish, because *Colette* was already parading toward the door. "Well, I guess that's it, then! I don't want to run the risk of having someone **STEAL** it!"

JULIe and the rest of the THEA SiSTERS were waiting in front of the academy with their snouts pressed against the window.

When they saw Colette strut out, they looked at one another in **wonder**.

A small crowd peered out the door of the fashion school. They followed Colette with their eyes as she **strode away**.

"**Give me five, Jules!**" exclaimed Pam enthusiastically, slapping her 🐾🐾🐾 against Julie's. "Next stop, Hollywood! Our Colette is a born actress!"

"The trap is set," said Violet **calmly**. "Now for the next part of the plan! We've got to keep our eyes on Colette. Let's see if the **THIEF** takes the **bait**."

IN THE
DEPARTMENT STORE

At this point, Colette had to **IMPROVISE**.

The mouselings had no way of knowing **if**, **when**, or **where** the **THIEF** would strike. It was up to Colette to make sure the thief had the right opportunity to steal the shawl. The tricky part was that the thief could absolutely not realize that it was a **TRAP**!

A chill went down Colette's tail. Where should she go? She decided to follow her instincts. And her instincts told her to head toward the closest department store. A large **CROWD** would be there: It seemed like an ideal place to **STEAL**—or rather, *let things be stolen*!

Pam couldn't believe her **EYES** when

she saw Colette go into one of Paris's **biggest** department stores. "What is she doing? She's going into a department store? It's so CROWDED, we'll lose her for sure!"

"No, not if we keep our eyes **open**," replied Violet.

Meanwhile, Colette had **GONE UP** the escalator. With all the shoppers milling around, it was impossible to tell if anyone was following her.

JULIE, *Nicky*, Pam, PAULINA, and **Violet** started after her. "She's going to the junior rodents department!" noted Paulina.

THE MOUSELINGS HAVE NOT SPOTTED THE THIEF.
DO YOU SEE HIM?

"How strange! I was sure Colette would head straight for the hardware department!" joked Pamela.

Despite her **stress**, Colette couldn't help oohing and aahing over some of the season's **newest** arrivals. *What a dream!* she thought when she spotted a cute top.

Then she remembered that she was there to have the shawl stolen. *Of course!* she thought. The best thing to do was *pretend* to

go **SHOPPING**! She had found the perfect
solution.

Colette was sure the THEA SISTERS were
nearby. So she grabbed a few tops to try on,
slipped into a dressing room, and hung the
shawl over the door. That way, whoever
was outside could take it.

She didn't need to wait long. One second
the shawl was there, and the next it had
vanished!

The THEA SISTERS saw a rodent with a trench coat, big dark **glasses**, and a hat **run away** with a bag in his paws.

He or she was completely UNRECOGNIZABLE.

They **STARTED** following the sneaky mouse.

THE HUNT IS ON!

Colette, JULIE, Nicky, Pamela, PAULINA, and **Violet** *rushed* out of the department store. But the THIEF was faster than they thought.

"He's going toward the SEINE!" Violet cried.

"The Pont* Alexandre III is nearby," Julie panted. "Maybe he's headed toward the other bank!"

The streets were so CROWDED it was hard to keep track of the THIEF. For a moment, the mouselings thought they'd lost SIGHT of him. The chase was a real tail-twister!

They scurried along and found themselves in an open square with very few houses. It seemed like the thief had VANISHED into

* *Pont* is French for "bridge."

thin air. He hadn't crossed the bridge, which was right in front of them. But the mouselings didn't see anyone on the **street** in either direction.

"The ladders!" shouted Colette, pointing to two ladders on the ends of the bridge. They led to the banks of the Seine.

Nicky peered over the river's edge. "Holey cheese! **There!** There he goes!"

She'd spotted the thief jumping on board a motorboat and zooming away at *FULL SPEED*.

"We've **LOST** him!" groaned Paulina. "The **tracker** can't cover long distances."

But Colette was not ready to give up. In fact, she was already *scampering* along the riverbank. "Look down there! It's a boat-rental shop! There's still HOPE!"

A CHASE ALONG THE SEINE!

JULIE and the other mouselings had never seen Colette so **determined**! Within moments, they had rented a motorboat and were HOT on the thief's trail. Colette was at the prow of the boat, pointing the way.

Violet was next to Colette, shouting directions. "CAREFUL of the barge on your right!"

Meanwhile, the *THIEF* had passed the Pont de l'Alma.

"Where do you think he, or she—it could be a female rodent—is headed?" Pamela asked Julie.

"I don't have the slightest idea!" she answered.

Pont de l'Alma, Passerelle Debilly, Pont d'Iéna—they passed bridge after bridge, but still the distance between the two **boats** had not changed. At the Pont de Bir-Hakeim, a **long** and NARROW island SPLIT the Seine into two canals.

Colette slowed down. She had to choose one canal. After a moment's hesitation, she chose the one on the right.

Soon an unexpected sight appeared before them—the **STATUE OF LIBERTY**?!?

"What is the Statue of Liberty doing here?!" cried Paulina in SURPRISE.

But Paulina's **CRY** was drowned out by Violet's: "Turn left! The **THIEF** is turning back!"

"He must have spotted us! He's trying to SHAKE us!" exclaimed Colette.

She started to turn around but had to

THE STATUE OF LIBERTY

From the Pont de Grenelle, which stretches over Île des Cygnes (Island of the Swans), you can see a miniature version of the Statue of Liberty. It was a gift to the people of Paris from a group of Americans living in Paris in 1889. The original statue was a gift from France to the United States to celebrate one hundred years of independence. It was unveiled in 1886.

pause to let a pontoon pass.

"**Au revoir**, shawl!" sighed Nicky.

"Don't say that yet!" said Paulina as she got out her MousePhone. "Let's see if my **tracker** works. We just have to stay close."

On the ᵗⁱⁿʸ screen, a piece of the Seine appeared, and on it a **red dot** was bouncing along quickly.

"**Got it!**" said Paulina with satisfaction.

A RED DOT ON
THE SCREEN

The red dot stopped suddenly.

"The THIEF has STEPPED OFF his boat," said Paulina.

"But where?" asked Colette.

"On the Right Bank!" cried Paulina. "Head toward Concorde Square!"

Colette steered the motorboat sharply toward the Right Bank. The mouselings ducked to avoid being SPLASHED.

"I'm getting a little sick of this cat-and-mouse game," sighed Nicky, wiping water from her snout.

As soon as Colette had tied up the boat, all six mouselings scurried out and started to run after the thief.

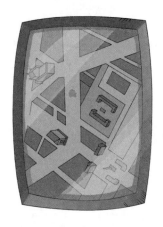

"He's on rue Royale!" yelled Paulina without taking her **EYES** off the MousePhone.

"He must be trying to lose us by **GETTING LOST** among the tourists!" said Nicky.

"He turned right," Paulina announced. "He's on Madeleine Boulevard."

"The OPERA!" Julie gasped, trying to catch her **breath**.

"So it's true!" Colette exclaimed. "The thief is going to the OPERA HOUSE! Just like the **MAP**!"

"**Greasy cat guts,** we were right!" said Pamela. "The **trEAsurE** is hidden in the theater!"

The **THIEF** figured that the mouselings had given up by now. There was no way they would have been able to **KEEP UP**

for so long. So he stopped **RUNNING**.

The THEA SISTERS arrived at the OPERA HOUSE just in time to see a **shadowy figure** turn down an alley and slip through a side entrance of the theater. The figure SLAMMED the door behind him.

Without pausing to form a plan, *Nicky*, **Violet**, PAULINA, *Colette*, *Pamela*, and JULIE followed him inside.

THE CHASE CONTINUED!

STAGE FRIGHT

The mouselings found themselves in a storage room filled with set designs and equipment. There were costumes, scenery, ropes, stage furniture, suits of armor, and curtains all around them.

In the **darkness**, Colette didn't realize that there was a box full of PROPS right next to her. She accidentally stuck her paw into it and stumbled, spilling the box's contents to the ground loudly.

CRAAAAASH!

"Crusty Camembert with croutons on top!" she cried in frustration.

"Colette, are you okay?" asked Violet, reaching out a paw to steady her friend.

"No, I'm not okay. Nothing is okay!"

CRAAAASH!

Colette said under her breath, holding back tears. "I twisted my ankle! *Ouch!*"

Meanwhile, Paulina was FRANTICALLY tinkering with her MousePhone. The **red dot** had disappeared from the screen. "I don't know where the **THIEF** went!" she whispered.

"Let's try this door," said Nicky. "It looks like the only way **out**, other than the way we came in."

They left the room and entered a **DIMLY LIT** corridor, which led to a **wooden staircase**. From there they found themselves onstage, behind the **curtains**. The mouselings grabbed one another's paws and held on tightly.

"Here it is! It's come back!" exclaimed Paulina, pointing to the **red dot**, which had reappeared on the MousePhone.

"Do you know where the **THIEF** is?" asked Colette.

PAULINA was having a hard time figuring it out. The theater's floor plan was very **COMPLEX**, with all its hallways, passages, **twisting** stairs, and storage areas.

"I'm not sure, but it seems like . . . maybe . . . well, I think he's right underneath us!" Paulina said.

CRACK!

At that moment, a **TRAPDOOR** burst open under their paws. Colette, JULIE, Nicky, Pamela, PAULINA, and **Violet** were falling down, down, down, down, down, down . . .

"**HELLLLLLLLLLLLLLLLP!**" they squeaked at the top of their lungs.

Trapdoors onstage are connected to walkways or elevators. They are used to help an actor or a singer make a sudden appearance. The singer or actor waits under the stage until he or she hears a cue, and then he or she makes an entrance.

WHAT A CRAFTY RODENT!

Colette, JULIE, Nicky, Pamela, PAULINA, and **Violet** fell on top of a pile of fabric, blankets, and mattresses.

"Well, that was lucky," Pam said.

"You call that **LUCKY**?" Nicky asked, rubbing her SORE tail. "Squeak for yourself! This thief is making me madder than a cat with a bad case of fleas!"

After they'd recovered from the shock of their fall, the mouselings untangled themselves from the scraps of fabric that had cushioned them.

The mouselings waited until their eyes grew accustomed to the DARK ROOM around them, then began to search for a way out.

After a moment, Pamela found a door. She jiggled the handle. "It's **LOCKED**. Does anyone have any idea how to open it?"

The mouselings looked around. The room was filled with a lot of **equipment**.

Nicky grabbed an **iron rod**. "Maybe we can use this to **BUST OPEN** the door. It doesn't seem very thick."

It was harder than they'd thought. But after a few minutes of pushing, Nicky, Pam, and Violet managed to break the lock.

The door opened onto the same **DIMLY LIT** hallway they had been in before.

"Wait!" cried Paulina suddenly, holding them back. "The **red dot** is back! I couldn't get a signal in the storage room, but out here I can track the thief again."

"Where is the thief, exactly?" Colette asked Paulina.

"He's climbing the **STAIRS**!" she answered.

Julie nodded. "Yes! There is a staircase that leads to the **costume** storage room! I've been there before. Professor Le Blanc took us to see it. Come on, it's this way!"

The mouselings **CLIMBED** the spiral staircase as quietly as possible.

There was a sudden noise from above—THUMP THUMP THUMP—and the mouselings stopped short.

"Those must be the pawsteps of the **THIEF**!" Colette whispered.

JULIE had reached the landing. The door at the top stood slightly ajar, and the room on the other side was **lit up**.

Julie **peeked** inside, opening the door slowly so as not to be seen. Then . . .

"**PROFESSOR LE BLANC!**" she shouted in *surprise*.

It was really him, her **kindest** professor, the one who had tried to encourage her during the most **DiFFiCULT** moments of the past few days!

In one **paw**, he held Colette's **Shawl**. In the other, he was holding a strange **PatC#WORK** quilt. It was made of many pieces of fabric all sewn together.

Julie was **frozen** in the doorway. She couldn't believe her **EYES**.

The professor didn't even try to defend himself. He just lowered his gaze and turned red with **shame**.

"I'm sorry, Julie!" he said. "I've been **TERRIBLE**. I ruined your work!"

"Oh, **nooooooo!**" groaned Colette.

The professor didn't have a

Pa**t**C✳**ШOГK** quilt in his paws—he was holding Julie's collection! It was cut into **PIECES** and patched together to create a **trEAsurE** map!

"I'm so ashamed!" the professor said, hanging his snout. "For years I have searched for that map; it has become an **OBSESSION**."

"But why?" asked Julie in a high squeak. "Why is that map so **IMPORTANT**?"

Professor Le Blanc didn't have the **COURAGE** to look Julie in the eye. "Do you remember my lecture about Pierre-Mouseon Fabriçon?"

"Who's he?" asked Pamela.

"He was a great fashion designer from the nineteenth century," Julie explained.

"The **greatest**!" Professor Le Blanc said, correcting her. "He was a **true genius**!"

P F

PiERRE-MOUSEON FABRiÇON

Talking about his obsession seemed to revive the professor. He launched into a history of Pierre-Mouseon Fabriçon's career.

"For years I have studied Fabriçon's sketches, trying to discover the secret of his spectacular and *sophisticated* clothing!" said Professor Le Blanc. "**FABRIÇON** was a genius. He created the most gorgeous gowns for the divas of the opera. And he also created special

looms on which he could weave uniquely Light fabrics to create pieces that became legendary for their *beauty*!"

The professor lowered his squeak. "But here's the TERRIBLE

thing: Nothing that **FABRIÇON** made still exists. Nothing!"

The THEA SISTERS stared at him in bewilderment. They were still angry, but they were starting to feel curious, too.

"Why?" asked Pam. "Were his gowns destroyed somehow?"

"They were hidden!" the professor said. "They are hidden *here*, in this THEATER, but *no one* knows where!"

"But now *you* know, right, **PROFESSOR**?" said Violet, pointing to the **multicolored** map made from Julie's clothes. "Now you have the **treAsure** map you've been searching for!"

Professor Le Blanc spread the **PatCHWORK** cloth across the table. One piece was still missing: Colette's Shawl.

"**FABRIÇON** created **extraordinary** evening gowns and stage costumes," the professor said. "The GREATEST singers in the world turned to him. He only made one-of-a-kind pieces, from precious materials and fabrics that he wove himself! He was VERY PROTECTIVE of his work. He had a workshop here, in this theater. No one was allowed in. That's how he protected his creations."

"I'll bet **FABRIÇON** didn't leave anything behind," Pam said. "So his work **DISAPPEARED** with him, right?"

The professor nodded. "Yes, his work disappeared with him. But he left a **MAP**."

"JULiE'S map!" exclaimed Paulina.

"A map that could be used to find his works. I have searched for it for **SO** long!" the professor lamented. He turned to Julie. "That day at the used-book stand, I was there, too. I had just found the right book,

with the **MAP** inside it. I had my **EYE** on it when you came along and took it **AWAY**! Of course, you had no idea of its significance. But at that moment it was like seeing years and years of my research go up in **smoke**."

A **silence** fell over the costume storage room. Everyone's eyes were glued to the **multicolored** fabric that extended across

the table: a strange **MAP** made of **CUT-UP** fabrics that led to a **treAsure** of clothing.

"**So what are we waiting for?**" Pamela blurted out. She couldn't stand sitting around doing nothing. "Let's look for the **SECRET** room!"

With that, Julie **grabbed** Colette's **shawl** and spread it out so that it matched up with the **design** on the map.

"Now it's complete!" she said, **EXAMiNiNG** it carefully.

The professor ran his **paws** along the fabric, recognizing the rooms and corridors of the **THEATER**. "The foyer . . . the stage . . . the rehearsal room . . . the dressing rooms . . . ," he murmured.

Parts of the Theater

1. **The entrance hall, or foyer:** The space just inside the entrance to the opera house, where the audience can mingle during intermission.
2. **The gallery:** The seats that are highest and farthest from the stage. These seats are also the least expensive.
3. **Box seats:** Open rooms that face the theater on various levels. They are designed to accommodate small groups of spectators.
4. **The front of the stage, or footlights:** The part of the stage that is closest to the audience.
5. **The proscenium:** The part of the stage where the action occurs.
6. **The orchestra pit:** The space reserved for the orchestra.
7. **The prompter's box:** An opening in the center of the footlights, where the prompter can sit hidden from the public by a small dome. (The prompter's job is to hold the script and remind the actors of their lines in case they forget them.)
8. **Theater stalls:** The lowest part of the theater reserved for the public. It is located right in front of the stage.

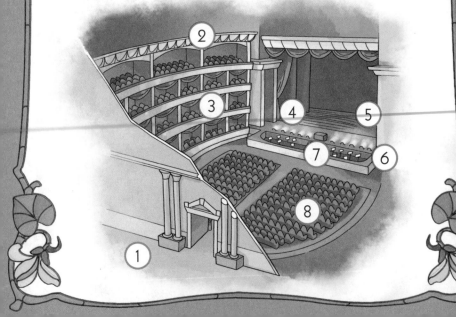

"Excuse me, but why don't we try doing this with the 𝔸ℂ𝕋𝕌𝔸𝕃 floor plan?" Paulina suggested, holding up her MousePhone.

"I don't think we'll need it," said Colette, pointing to a strange symbol on the map. "Look at this. It's mixed in with all the other notes on the **MAP**, but it isn't a door or a room."

"What is it?" asked *Nicky*. She was on the other side of the **table**, so she could see the symbol only upside down.

"It looks like initials," said Colette.

"A **P** and an **F** put together!" said Julie.

"Those are **PIERRE-MOUSEON FABRIÇON'S** initials!" the professor exclaimed.

THE SECRET OF THE SPHINX

Professor Le Blanc had no doubt: The initials showed where Pierre-Mouseon Fabriçon's OLD workshop was hidden. That was where the treAsure would be!

The professor knew the THEATER well. He led the little group to a LONG and NARROW room with a very high ceiling. It was the storage room for old backdrops and plaster statues.

A dusty light filtered in from a dormer window. There were no doors other than the one they had used to enter.

"It's a DEAD END!" said Julie, disappointed.

At that moment, Pam let out a high-pitched squeak: "EEEEEEEEEEEEEEEEEEEEEEK!"

She had seen a SPIDER on the ground. Pam was terrified of bugs of all kinds.

Her scream made everyone jump in fright, including the SPIDER. The small, scared arthropod hid behind a huge plaster sphinx leaning against one wall.

Professor Le Blanc checked the MAP. "The treAsure—or rather, Pierre-Mouseon Fabriçon's SECRET ROOM —

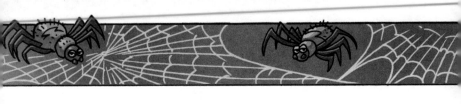

should be hidden *here*, right behind the **plaster** sphinx!"

The professor rolled up his sleeves and began pushing the statue. But it seemed to be nailed to the ground.

Nicky and Paulina came to his **aid**, as did Violet, Julie, Pam, and Colette. Who knew how long it had been since the sphinx had been moved!

"**CHEESECAKE!** This thing is heavier than a **BOULDER** covered with **moldy cheese**!" cried Nicky.

Very slowly, the statue began to budge. As it did, the SPiDeR disappeared into a crack between the wall and the floor. A stream of light came from below.

The wall was made of **WOOD**, and it was hiding a closed door with a **RUSTY LOCK**.

With one more determined **SHOVE**, the door burst open.

CRACK!

Concealed behind a thick curtain of SPIDERWEBS, a vast two-story room lay before them. In the middle was a **long** table with two **PAPER PATTERNS** lying open, ready to be used. On the side was a big **loom**, and around it small mannequins dressed in different types of costumes. A thick layer of **dust** covered everything.

Was this the **treAsure** Professor Le Blanc had been looking for?

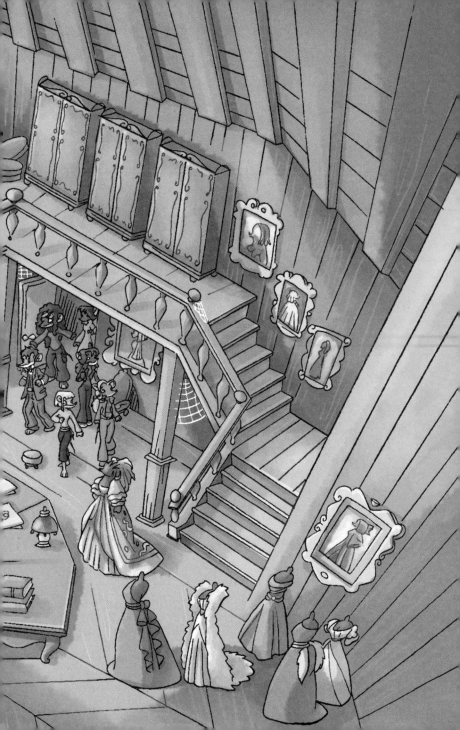

THE TREASURE

Professor Le Blanc couldn't believe his eyes: In front of him was the *treasure* he had been *chasing* for many years. He hesitated for a moment, then **APPROACHED** a mannequin. He recognized the costume instantly: It was from *Semiramide*! There wasn't a single book about the HISTORY OF FASHION that didn't mention it! "Light as the wings of a butterfly, sparkling with silk and strings of **GOLD** laced together"— that was how the newspapers of the day had described it.

Professor Le Blanc extended his paw to wipe some dust off the sleeve . . .

But as soon as his fingers touched the fabric, the delicate lace began to crumble.

"**NOOOOOOOOOOOOOOOOOOO!**" cried the professor.

More than a century of neglect had YELLOWED the fabric, **faded** the colors, corroded the stitching, and deprived the lavish dresses in the room of their splendor.

SEMIRAMIDE

Semiramide is a lyric opera in two acts with a historic setting. The music is by Gioacchino Rossini, and the libretto by Gaetano Rossi. It's based on Voltaire's tragedy *Semiramis*, which tells the story of the successor to the throne in Babylon, where Semiramide is queen.

Semiramide was first performed at La Fenice theater in Venice in February 1823.

Julie examined the LOOM Fabriçon had used to create his precious fabrics. The EQUIPMENT seemed to be in good shape.

But the THEA SISTERS looked around in despair. Everyone's thoughts could be summed up in three words: **What a disappointment!**

Pamela didn't want to believe it. She ran up some stairs that led to a loft. There were closets up there. SURELY they must hold some precious objects.

She opened the first one and . . .
"**EEEEEEEEEEEEK!**"

She was overwhelmed by a cloud of moths.
The closets had been invaded by the insects!
Whatever clothing or fabric they had once
held had long been **destroyed**.

"It's all lost! **Lost!**" lamented the
professor.

Colette lost her **patience**. "**Easy** for you to squeak!" she said, wagging a finger at him. "**FABRIÇON'S** clothes were destroyed by moths, but Julie's clothes were **destroyed** by you!"

The professor **STAGGERED** under the weight of her accusation.

It was Julie who consoled him. "It's okay, Professor. It doesn't matter! Discovering

Fabriçon's workshop is still an IMPORTANT milestone in the history of fashion. And the LOOM is still intact."

Colette, on the other paw, was not as forgiving. "It's not enough! Your professor is a THIEF! He ruined your fashion show!"

"But, Colette . . . ," Julie began.

Professor Le Blanc grabbed her paw. "Your cousin is right. I behaved terribly. And I am most ashamed at having betrayed your trust, Julie."

"That's MORE LIKE IT!" Colette declared. "But I don't think the police are interested in your BETRAYAL of trust! Being sorry is important, but Julie can't send an apology down the ratwalk!"

"SO what do you suggest, Colette?" asked Pam, who was still trying to shake the moths from her fur.

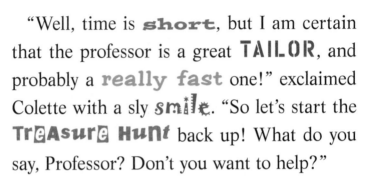

"Well, time is **short**, but I am certain that the professor is a great **TAILOR**, and probably a **really fast** one!" exclaimed Colette with a sly **smile**. "So let's start the **Treasure Hunt** back up! What do you say, Professor? Don't you want to help?"

The professor **nodded** slowly. The mouselings could tell he was **heartbroken** with disappointment, but it was clear he wanted to make up for the problems he had caused Julie.

"**ALL RIGHT, THEN!**" declared Colette. "Let's scurry back to the **ACADEMY**. We've got lots to do. Let's MAKE IT WORK, mouselings!"

IN THE SHADOW OF THE EIFFEL TOWER

A few days later, the night of the *fashion show* arrived.

The sky was calm, but the atmosphere was **electric**!

The space under the *Eiffel Tower* had been transformed by a ratwalk, **spotlights**, *flowers*, carpets, steps, chairs for the guests, and reserved areas for the workers. Journalists and

photographers from the most famous **FASHION MAGAZINES** had come to see the new designers' work.

Julie's name appeared in the program, next to the name of her collection: **TrEAsurE HuNt**. But no one had seen her arrive.

One after the other, the new graduates presented their **creations**.

Wei and **Mei's** paper clothes sparked a lot of **curiosity**. But Fernando's **METALLIC DESIGNS** got more **APPLAUSE**.

Leon Paella's sparkly **robots** were beginning their strut down the ratwalk when there was a **fuss** behind the curtains.

A small truck sped to the backstage area, and out stepped . . .

"JULie?!" exclaimed Wanda in disbelief.

Julie looked **pale** and tense, as if she hadn't gotten any **sleep** in a while.

Her classmates gathered around her and **bombarded** her with questions.

"Did they catch the *THIEF*?"

"Will you be showing your work?"

"Did you get your CLOTHES back?"

"Not exactly," Julie replied. "But I am ready to show my stuff tonight!"

The other *students* in her class gathered around and hugged her.

"Good for you, JULIE!"

"You're so **BRAVE**!"

"Break a paw!"

They hadn't stopped cheering her on when her name was called on the **ratwalk**.

Soon all the SPOTLIGHTS were on Julie.

Nervously, Julie took her place behind the microphone. "My collection is called TrEAsurE HuNt," she began. As she squeaked, the music began to play. SURPRISE — Pamela appeared on the ratwalk!

"Pamela is wearing a piece called Africa," Julie continued. "Traditional jewelry completes her look."

Pamela walked a little awkwardly, but she had a huge smile on her snout. Then it was Nicky's turn.

"Nicky is wearing AUSTRALIA, with a top and gloves made of chiffon," Julie announced. "While PAULINA"—at that moment, she, too, emerged from behind the curtains—"is wearing a number called South America, with a high collar made of taffeta."

Then it was Violet's turn. "Violet is wearing ASIA, a silk dress with a rhinestone belt around her hips. And finally, we have Europe, also known as Paris Nights. . . ."

Colette came out. She was dressed in PINK from snout to paw. And she was stunning!

The crowd gave Julie's collection a standing ovation. They rose to their paws, **clapping** as hard as they could.

Professor Le Blanc, who was watching from the front row, *smiled* at Julie. He had ruined her collection, but it was thanks to his help that Julie was able to sew new clothes. And they were even more **BEAUTIFUL** than the originals!

JULIE had used **SCRAPS** from the first collection, but the fabric and the **printed** designs were different. Each piece represented a **MAP** of the continent where one of the THEA SISTERS was born.

Julie concluded her presentation. "I called this collection **Treasure Hunt** because it contains the most precious *treasure* of all: **FRIENDSHIP**! These *five mouselings* come from five different continents, and they love each other like sisters! Friendship is the most valuable **trEAsurE**, because it can **unite** people from all over the WORLD!"

At that point the audience burst into applause again. Even Julie's classmates joined in, ***moved*** by her speech.

Julie ran to hug her *friends*. "Thanks, Colette! Thanks, mouselings! I don't know what I would have done without you!"

"Friends together! Mice forever!" Nicky cried.

Professor Le Blanc approached Julie, embarrassed. "I wanted you to know that I'm turning myself in to the **POLICE**. What I did was wrong. Can you ever **forgive** me?"

Julie smiled and squeezed the professor's **paw**. "All is forgiven! Plus, **LOOK**: My collection is even more amazing than before, because it was made with *love*!"

There was no doubt: JULie was the true **winner** of the fashion show!

And that, dear readers, concludes the *Paris adventure* of our friends the THEA SiSTERS!

They were more than friends. They were sisters!

THEA SISTERS

Thea Stilton

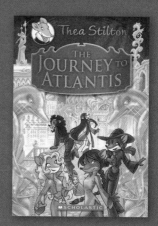

Secret Fairies

Don't miss any of these exciting series featuring the Thea Sisters!

Treasure Seekers

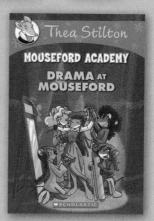

Mouseford Academy

Don't miss any of these exciting Thea Sisters adventures!

Thea Stilton and the Dragon's Code

Thea Stilton and the Mountain of Fire

Thea Stilton and the Ghost of the Shipwreck

Thea Stilton and the Secret City

Thea Stilton and the Mystery in Paris

Thea Stilton and the Cherry Blossom Adventure

Thea Stilton and the Star Castaways

Thea Stilton: Big Trouble in the Big Apple

Thea Stilton and the Ice Treasure

Thea Stilton and the Secret of the Old Castle

Thea Stilton and the Blue Scarab Hunt

Thea Stilton and the Prince's Emerald

Thea Stilton and the Mystery on the Orient Express

Thea Stilton and the Dancing Shadows

Thea Stilton and the Legend of the Fire Flowers

Thea Stilton and the Spanish Dance Mission

**Thea Stilton and the
Journey to the Lion's Den**

**Thea Stilton and the
Great Tulip Heist**

**Thea Stilton and the
Chocolate Sabotage**

**Thea Stilton and the
Missing Myth**

**Thea Stilton and the
Lost Letters**

**Thea Stilton and the
Tropical Treasure**

**Thea Stilton and the
Hollywood Hoax**

**Thea Stilton and the
Madagascar Madness**

**Thea Stilton and the
Frozen Fiasco**

**Thea Stilton and the
Venice Masquerade**

**Thea Stilton and the
Niagara Splash**

**Thea Stilton and the
Riddle of the Ruins**

**Thea Stilton and the
Phantom of the Orchestra**

**Thea Stilton and the
Black Forest Burglary**

**Thea Stilton and the
Race for the Gold**

Don't miss a single fabumouse adventure!

Up Next:

Don't miss any of my adventures in the Kingdom of Fantasy!

THE KINGDOM OF FANTASY

THE QUEST FOR PARADISE:
THE RETURN TO THE KINGDOM OF FANTASY

THE AMAZING VOYAGE:
THE THIRD ADVENTURE IN THE KINGDOM OF FANTASY

THE DRAGON PROPHECY:
THE FOURTH ADVENTURE IN THE KINGDOM OF FANTASY

THE VOLCANO OF FIRE:
THE FIFTH ADVENTURE IN THE KINGDOM OF FANTASY

THE SEARCH FOR TREASURE:
THE SIXTH ADVENTURE IN THE KINGDOM OF FANTASY

THE ENCHANTED CHARMS:
THE SEVENTH ADVENTURE IN THE KINGDOM OF FANTASY

THE PHOENIX OF DESTINY:
AN EPIC KINGDOM OF FANTASY ADVENTURE

THE HOUR OF MAGIC:
THE EIGHTH ADVENTURE IN THE KINGDOM OF FANTASY

THE WIZARD'S WAND:
THE NINTH ADVENTURE IN THE KINGDOM OF FANTASY

THE SHIP OF SECRETS:
THE TENTH ADVENTURE IN THE KINGDOM OF FANTASY

THE DRAGON OF FORTUNE:
AN EPIC KINGDOM OF FANTASY ADVENTURE

THE GUARDIAN OF THE REALM:
THE ELEVENTH ADVENTURE IN THE KINGDOM OF FANTASY

THE ISLAND OF DRAGONS:
THE TWELFTH ADVENTURE IN THE KINGDOM OF FANTASY

Visit Geronimo in every universe!

Spacemice
Geronimo Stiltonix and his crew are out of this world!

Cavemice
Geronimo Stiltonoot, an ancient ancestor, is friends with the dinosaurs in the Stone Age!

Micekings
Geronimo Stiltonord lives amongst the dragons in the ancient far north!

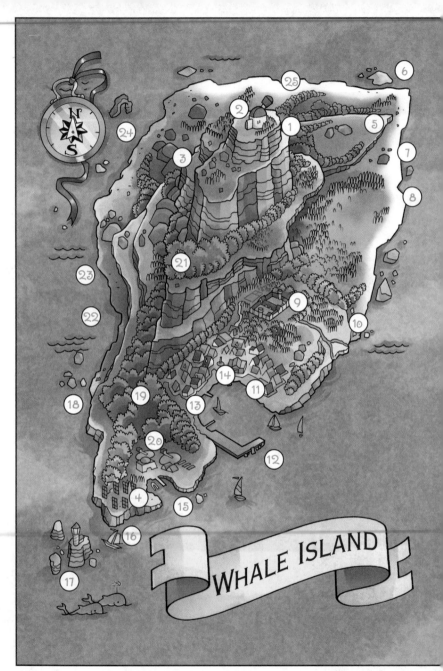

WHALE ISLAND

MAP OF WHALE ISLAND

1. Falcon Peak
2. Observatory
3. Mount Landslide
4. Solar Energy Plant
5. Ram Plain
6. Very Windy Point
7. Turtle Beach
8. Beachy Beach
9. Mouseford Academy
10. Kneecap River
11. Mariner's Inn
12. Port
13. Squid House
14. Town Square
15. Butterfly Bay
16. Mussel Point
17. Lighthouse Cliff
18. Pelican Cliff
19. Nightingale Woods
20. Marine Biology Lab
21. Hawk Woods
22. Windy Grotto
23. Seal Grotto
24. Seagulls Bay
25. Seashell Beach

THANKS FOR READING, AND GOOD-BYE UNTIL OUR NEXT ADVENTURE!